This **Walker** book

belongs to:

For Sophie xxx

First published 2023 by Walker Books Ltd, 87 Vauxhall Walk, London SE11 5HJ

This edition published 2024

2 4 6 8 10 9 7 5 3 1

© 2023 Catherine Rayner

The right of Catherine Rayner to be identified as author of this work has been asserted
in accordance with the Copyright, Designs and Patents Act 1988

This book has been typeset in Baskerville

Printed in China

British Library Cataloguing in Publication Data: a catalogue record for this book
is available from the British Library

ISBN 978-1-5295-1718-7

www.walker.co.uk

WALKER BOOKS
AND SUBSIDIARIES

LONDON • BOSTON • SYDNEY • AUCKLAND

Molly, Olive & Dexter
The Guessing Game
Catherine Rayner

At the bottom of the garden, there's an oak tree.

It's home to Molly the hare, Olive the owl and Dexter the fox.

Olive loves guessing games.

"Shall we play GUESS WHAT?" she asks.

"All right," says Dexter.

"Guess what I'm thinking about."

"Aha!" Molly bounces up and down. "It's … the **SKY**!"

"How did you know?" asks Dexter, puzzled.

"Oh, Dexter!" Olive hoots with laughter. "You were looking right at it. Now it's your turn, Molly."

"I'm ready," says Molly. "Guess what I'm thinking about."

"Is it grass?" asks Olive.

Molly nods. "How did you know?"

"Easy," says Olive. "Your mouth is full of it!"

"My turn." Olive swoops through
the air. "I'm thinking about **TWO**
things at the same time!"

"Hmmm." Dexter looks around.

"Is it those **TWO** golden leaves?"

"No," says Olive. "Try again!"

"How about those **TWO** clouds?" asks Molly.

"No," says Olive. "Try again!"

"We're not doing very well," says Dexter.

"Can you give us a clue?"

"The **TWO** things I'm thinking about are … very near by," Olive tells them.

"What about those

TWO butterflies?" asks Molly.

"No," says Olive. "Try again!"

"Here's another clue," she adds. "The **TWO** things I'm thinking about are *lovely*."

"Now I've got it!" Dexter cries. "**TWO** … flowers!"

"No," says Olive. "But keep trying."

"It's too hard," says Molly. "I give up."

"Think about something even *lovelier* than flowers," says Olive.

"NOTHING is lovelier than flowers," grumbles Dexter.

"You're too good at this game," huffs Molly. "It's not fair."

"But guessing is the game!" says Olive. "Getting it wrong is part of the fun. Come on. I'm thinking about the two loveliest things in the world … and you KNOW the answer."

Molly sighs.

Dexter grumps.

Molly frowns.

Dexter scowls.

Then Molly and Dexter look at each other.

"Oh!" says Molly.

"Oh!" says Dexter. "We CAN think of two lovely things."

"That's it!" Olive cries. "You worked it out together.

I'm thinking about…"

"The two of you!"

"Hooray! We all won!" says Dexter. "This game is lovely."

"It's the loveliest game in the world," says Molly.

And before long they settle under the oak tree
at the bottom of the garden for a nice long nap.

Three best friends.

Also in this series:

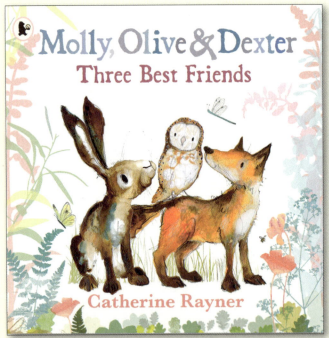

ISBN: 978-1-5295-1756-9

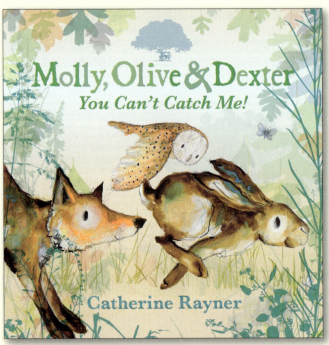

ISBN: 978-1-5295-0155-1

Available from all good booksellers

www.walker.co.uk